Rain City Cats

Rain City Cats

A True International Adventure

by Kiska, the Cat
(as told to Pamela Bauer Mueller)

PIÑATA PUBLISHING

Piñata Publishing
112 Dunbarton Drive
St. Simons Island, GA 31522
912-638-2676
www.kiskalore.com

CANADIAN CATALOGUING IN PUBLICATION
Mueller, Pamela Bauer
  Rain city cats

ISBN: 0-9685097-1-1

  1. Cats—Juvenile fiction. I. Title.
P27.B324RA2000   J813´54   C00-910508-5

Library of Congress Card Number: 00-91222

Typeset by the Vancouver Desktop Publishing Centre
Printed and bound in Canada by Ray Hignell Services Inc.

I dedicate this book to my
partner and husband, Michael,
whose love has nourished and sustained me.
Thank you for your patience,
unconditional support and above all,
for your steadfast faith in my work.

Acknowledgments

I would like to gratefully recognize the following people who supported and encouraged me throughout the writing of the sequel to *The Bumpedy Road*, entitled *Rain City Cats*.

A very special thank you to Naomi Weiler. I am truly blessed to have her as my illustrator and friend. Naomi, thanks for the laughter. You made *Rain City Cats* a complete sensory experience.

Phyllis Bauer, my incredible mother, who not only is my best customer, sharing *The Bumpedy Road* with her extensive circle of friends, but also strengthens my convictions through her examples.

Miss Cassandra and Miss Ticiana, my grown up daughters, and their "keeper spouses", Dan and Ted. Each one of them continues to inspire and enlighten me through their solid faith and love of life.

My marvelous friends Mimi Cummings and Dennis Mulligan, who offered me the peace of their seaside home to complete the final revisions of *Rain City Cats*.

The Barens family: Marke, June, Nicke and Shawne. Our dearest Canadian friends lived much of this book with us, and deserve a great deal of credit for making our experiences in Canada so unique.

Bob and Mel, Ashleigh and Devin Herbert: our friendly next door neighbors who lovingly cared for our cats in our absence. And because of these "excellent neighbors," we tore down our fence!

Our very special Canadian friends who make up our Alpha group: Karen and Rick, Eleanor and Gary, John and Wendy, Dean and Kari, and Christy and Dave. Thank you for your camaraderie and your wisdom.

Roberta, Terri, Robert, Cherie, Rob, and the other local bookstore representatives who gave me the opportunity to speak, sign and sell my first published book. Many heartfelt thanks to each one of you!

Tracy Johnson, the "web maker" who so patiently executed the many changes we requested as our business grew. Thanks for your innovative work!

Our beloved granddaughter Marlena Grace, for enriching our lives and loving our book.

Kudos to Patty Osborne, who once again created calm and cheerful order out of chaos.

My husband Michael, the best person I know. Thank you for being there for me each and every day!

Prologue

In this sequel to **The Bumpedy Road**, Kiska moves far away from her homeland in Mexico. In her first book she wrote about following her family to the United States. In this book she will accompany them on their next move to Canada. Her beloved Miss Cassandra and Miss Ticiana have grown into lovely young adults with lives of their own. Kiska now begins a new facet of her life and adds new pieces to her own puzzle.

One of the advantages of writing is becoming someone else: climbing inside someone else's skin and listening to another's heart. By imagining part of myself into a cat I can enable Kiska to imagine part of herself into a human. That's where our magical relationship begins, and that is how we can communicate to author a book.

In **Rain City Cats** Kiska discovers that her needs have changed as she copes with new beginnings. Armed with curiosity and resolve, she searches for her niche in British Columbia. In this, her Canadian story, she entertains, educates and touches us once again. Kiska articulates the things that we have all felt, but she speaks with feline wisdom and clarity. Her understanding of the human character is amusing, poignant, and endearing as she narrates the struggles and riches of her life. Once again, I am honored to be her spokesperson.

Pamela Bauer Mueller

Contents

RAIN CITY CATS

Rain city cats
Walkin' in the rain
Gotta find some shelter
'fore they go insane...

(chorus) cause they bin' walkin'
they bin' walkin'
since they started to roam,
they bin' walkin'
they bin' walkin'
now they wanna go home.

Rain city cats
walkin' in a storm
Trying to find a fire
So they can get warm...

(chorus)
Rain city cats
packin' up their bags
gonna fly somewhere
They can dry their rags...

(chorus)
... they bin' walkin', they bin' walkin'
now they wanna go home!

—Naomi Marie Werly

Where Am I?

Where am I? It's an odd feeling for a cat to be disoriented, but I am. How many hours ago was I let outside to explore this new place? And where are they? I'm very confused, and a bit frightened, which is also an unusual situation for me.

The sun is going down and the cool night air is settling around me, so I know I've been here many hours. Where are the Mistress and Miss Ticiana? I am huddled under a bush looking at what I think is our new house, but I'm not sure. I do not recognize anything around me. I've never been here before! This is truly disturbing, and I am losing my patience.

Just yesterday I was hiding under the bed, listening to the noisy strangers unloading furniture, unpacking boxes and disrupting my peace. The Mistress and Miss Ticiana were far too busy to look out for my comforts, but hearing their voices calmed me somewhat, enough to nap throughout the day. Come to think of it, I didn't eat until late afternoon, when I finally crawled out to investigate the silence. It was then that Miss Ticiana scooped me up in her arms and asked me if I liked our new house.

How did she expect me to respond? I was hungry, annoyed that I had been ignored all day, and feeling isolated from everything I knew. I did much prefer this large space to the car trip, however. Even yesterday they had me in the car, bringing me from the hotel room (which I'd grown to appreciate) to this large house, which I've been told is our new home. I did notice that it smelled wonderfully of pine trees, fresh running water, and a bird sanctuary, but as yet I had not ventured outdoors.

Now I hear the approach of two dogs and I crouch lower into the bushes. They smell my presence but are playing with a young boy so I won't be bothered.

From the empty feeling in my stomach, I think I've been outside too many hours. My family would never do this to me. I fear something has happened to them! Cats don't usually worry, because we are in control of our situations, but I'm worrying now.

I've lost concept of time this summer. How long ago did the Mistress, Mr. Mike and I leave San Diego in her cramped convertible? What a trip that was! I meowed and fussed the entire trip until I grew hoarse. We made stops along the way to visit relatives, so I had some breaks, but I was happy to reach our destination. From listening to conversations I realized we were moving to Canada, where the Mistress was relocating for her government job. Was that a month ago?

I closed my eyes and longed for the comfort and warmth of our hotel room, where we had been living for about a month. Each day the Mistress went to work, but soon returned to pamper and indulge me. It was just the two of us, and I received my worthy attention. Then Miss Ticiana arrived, and she cared for me while her mother was working. Everything was going so well until yesterday, when I was packed into my carrier and driven here. Even last night I snuggled under the covers with Miss Ticiana, and thought all would be well. But now I'm alone, worried, and wondering what has happened to my beloved family.

I will imagine drawing a white circle around them to keep them safe. That thought comforts me. Now I think I will try to take a short nap, which will conserve my energy and allow me to dream.

Dreaming

I was dreaming about my kittenhood, snuggled warm next to my brother, Canica. We grew up together in a town called Contadero, about half an hour's car ride from Mexico City. Our house was situated in a beautiful tree lined compound, with a forest directly behind. There were flowers, forts, playground equipment, and animals everywhere. Canica and I joined the other cats and dogs and the children in games of hide and seek and tag. When we tired of that, we visited the chicken farm, located at the entrance of our housing compound. We so enjoyed scaring the old hens and chasing the chicks but we would never hurt them even if we could catch them. This was done "after hours," since we were not allowed in there and very seldom managed to stay more than minutes.

In this dream I was reliving one day when Miss Ticiana, then eight years old, and Miss Cassandra, eleven, were trying to put rabbit leashes on Canica and me. We wanted no part of this nonsense, but they were our playmates and were trying so earnestly to harness us and walk us around the compound. Of course, even as kittens, we were embarrassed to have our animal friends watching this. So we decided to pretend that the leashes were "our" ideas. We stopped struggling and, for just that day, allowed our young owners to lead us around the grassy hills on leashes. With heads held high and tails straight up, we paraded back and forth for all to see. The look of surprise in the eyes of the neighbors' cats and dogs was well worth the discomfort!

Canica and I, Miss Cassandra and Miss Ticiana, and the Mistress and the Master enjoyed this idyllic living for more than three years. Sadly for all of us the Mistress and the Master divorced, so the Mistress brought us and her daughters to San Diego to start over. We all had culture shock for some time, but we cats seemed to recover more quickly than our owners did. After exploring the neighborhood and establishing new contacts, we urged our young ladies to do the same. We nurtured them, comforted them at night, and took great pride in watching them blossom and grow. The Mistress also suffered and struggled to find work. We watched over her and imagined protecting her with our affection whenever she went out. We know it worked, because she always returned safely, and soon began a new career working for the government.

So many wonderful memories of those days return to me in dreams. Dreams are why cats sleep so much, you know. We can traverse moments, even years, by

just closing our eyes. We travel back and visit our friends and loved ones by directing our thoughts a few seconds before we sleep. Even though we are now apart I can visit my brother Canica almost daily, and I'm sure he visits me in his dreams. I don't know exactly where he is, but I see him often on television. You see, Canica, always the restless leader, left us to become an animal actor! As sad as it was for me to let him go to Los Angeles without me, I knew he needed to follow his dream. We are all very proud of him, and he always waves to us and winks at the end of his cat food commercial.

The days passed and the girls were growing up. Miss Cassandra graduated from high school and went away to college. Canica had already found his way to a Hollywood career. Miss Ticiana returned to Mexico to study for a year and live with her father. The Mistress and I stayed together, sharing our lives with new friends, both animal and human. Her boyfriend, Mr. Mike, had just moved to San Diego, and was quickly accepted and respected by the girls and me.

Life was comfortable and good. Proms, graduations and family gatherings became pivotal events during one particular year. And then Miss Cassandra chose that same summer to have her wedding! Seeing her so radiant in her wedding gown brought tears to my eyes. How I wished that Canica could have been there to share it with me.

Just as we recuperated from so many events, we were moving again! The Mistress was offered the opportunity to go on foreign assignment to Vancouver, British Columbia, and felt the timing was perfect. She explained all this to me, and I smiled at her through half moon eyes, showing my acceptance. I was happy to follow her wherever her path led us. We both knew I would not be happy traveling by car, but she told me we could go slowly and make many stops. Ay yi yi! What a trip that was! Perhaps I should share it with you, and I will, after I finish my dream.

There are people who reshape the world by force or argument, but the cat just lies there, dozing, and the world quietly reshapes itself to suit his comfort and convenience.

Allen and Ivy Dodd, American writers

3

The "NAFTA" Cat

We left San Diego one fine summer morning. Mr. Mike was driving with the Mistress at his side, and I was at her feet on the floor in my carrier. The car was packed to the brim, with barely enough open space to see through the back window. I started crying the moment the car moved, meowing in many keys, over and over again. My series of protestations began from anxiety, but progressed to annoyance, despair and finally, defeat. Cats have many different tones of speech, from a quiet "mew" to a desperate "YEOW!" Before we reached our first night's destination, I was almost hoarse from howling. Mr. Mike was suggesting that I should be set free to roam the car in order to calm down. The Mistress was pleading with me to settle down and trying her best to calm me.

If cats are supposed to like small, sheltered spaces, then why was I so miserable? First of all, cats love confined spaces chosen by them. We like to go behind dressers and look for a drawer to crawl into. We then nestle between sweaters and socks and are perfectly content. We thoroughly dislike being forced into small spaces without windows on all four sides. Cats hate being subjected to tunnel vision. Our entire survival depends on seeing all around us, so we object to riding many hours in a cage with one tiny window.

The following day we continued up the California coastline. They wanted to enjoy the scenic route, but soon regretted it because of my protestations. The Mistress had bought me a purple harness and matching leash and once again they assumed that I would walk around with them and take my potty breaks on demand at their rest stops. Each time they put this contraption over my head, I squirmed and fought and cried. When they tugged the leash for me to walk forward, I lay down. One of them would pick me up and set me back on my feet, and I would topple over and lay inert. I'm not sure what their point was but after this trip they never tried to walk me on a leash again.

That night we went to my dear Miss Cassandra's house, where I was subjected to yet another cat! This one, Bambina, was young but spooked by my entrance into her domain. She spent that night either hissing at me or sneaking up behind me. Needless to say I hardly slept at all. My poor Miss Cassandra tried to ease my discomfort, but for once I could not respond to her kindness.

Finally we reached Oregon where we stayed two days with the Mistress's mother, Phyllis. She had a large house in a resort community, surrounded by woods. The Mistress tied my leash to a tree and left me to walk about and explore. They all sat outside on the deck and talked, presumably watching me enjoy my "freedom." It took me about five minutes to figure out how to slip out of the collar. Once free, away I went! Several minutes passed until they discovered that I was gone! Suddenly all three of them were

searching for me everywhere. My intention was not to run away, only to explore for a while and then return. But when I heard them calling for me, I slowly found my way back to the Mistress. How happy they all were to see me, and how I basked in the adoration that I received.

The next day we stopped at the Mistress's sister Rebecca's home where her two small children, Marshall and Clara, lovingly assaulted me. This only added to my state of discontent, but by then I was quite exhausted. I was ready for this journey to end. So were the Mistress and her boyfriend, as I now began to hear tones of quibbling and impatience from both of them.

Soon we reached the border of the United States and Canada. They explained to the Canadian border officials that the Mistress was going to work for the United States government and would be living in Canada. She told them I was a NAFTA (North American Free Trade Agreement) cat, which I learned was allowed duty free entry under Article 415 of the NAFTA Treaty. The brief explanation given was that I was "an article or good" born in Mexico, raised in the United States, and bound for Canada. I found myself speechless for the first time during the entire trip!

Of all God's creatures, there is only one that cannot be made the slave of the leash. That one is the cat. If man could be crossed with a cat, it would improve man, but it would deteriorate the cat.

Mark Twain, American writer

4
Rescued!

Soft summer winds begin to blow, and I open an eye to try to resolve my situation. While I was dreaming, things were peaceful. When I awakened, I became forlorn and agitated, knowing that things were not right. I feel lost and out of control, and wonder if my family has forgotten me. Logically, this could not be. Just the night before the Mistress had cooked chicken hearts for me, knowing that it was my first night in another "new house." She would not have abandoned me, and I knew this. But why was I still outside, late at night, trying to find my house? I close my eyes and decide that this problem could be resolved by sleeping once again.

I remembered that morning. I heard the alarm going off early, and noticed that the Mistress and Miss Ticiana dressed hurriedly and prepared to leave. They must have thought I would like to do my business outdoors, because they opened the door and put me out. It was still early and no one else was around, so I tentatively ventured out to explore. At this point I heard the car starting up and off they drove! I was still outdoors and wondering if they remembered, but I was not worried because they had left me for short periods before and returned to bring me back indoors. So I wandered about and checked out my new environment.

There was a great deal of land behind the house, including a tennis court, swimming pool, something that looked like a golf course, a barn, a merry-go-round and a pond. Actually, what really held my interest was the sound of the many different birds chirping, singing, and squawking. I followed the sounds and, to my astonishment, saw several birds that I had never seen in all my bird watching moments in Mexico or San Diego!

After a while, a medium sized sheltie sheep dog came bounding out of the house next door and began barking furiously, causing quite a ruckus. He sent me up a tree where I stayed until his family retrieved him. What a yapper he was, and when I eventually eased my way down that tree, I had a headache. I wandered about, looking for an entrance to my new house. Time went by, day fell into dusk, and no one returned. There was no sign of my family, or anyone else to open a door. I grew worried and began to pace, walking about in circles. I must have crossed the street in my confusion, because I finally ended up falling asleep under a bush.

I must be in a very deep sleep now because I am hearing the familiar "kitty, kitty, come here Kiska baby" being chanted over and over again. How sweet these sounds are to my ears! In my mind's eye, I can see the Mistress and Miss Ticiana with outstretched arms searching for me. I want to get up and run to them, but I am asleep, so I cannot move. But even in my dream I call out to them. That "meow" wakes me up, and I DO hear their voices! I shake my head and stand up, to make sure that I am no longer dreaming! Slowly, I open my mouth and utter a weak and mournful "yowl." In seconds, I see the Mistress and

Miss Ticiana rushing across the street and feel them swooping me into their arms, smothering me with kisses. I am so happy I can only respond with purrs and smiles. They carry me to our new house, and we spend the late hours cuddled together. They also give me an explanation of how they took a tour to Vancouver Island and did not realize that I was outside until their ferry landed. By then, there was no way to return and let me in. I listen, and lovingly wash their beautiful faces with my tongue, letting them know that they are forgiven.

With the qualities of cleanliness, affection, patience, dignity, and courage that cats have, how many of us, I ask you, would be capable of becoming cats?

Fernand Mery, French writer

My "Canada Place"

We were living in a house in an area called Crescent Beach, in British Columbia, Canada. A strange phenomenon happened to me in this place. I became an "indoor cat," something I had never been before. I cannot blame it on the weather, because I arrived during the summer months, which were warm and beautiful. Perhaps it was a result of the month's stay in the hotel, where I perched on a balcony and watched the world go by. Maybe it was due to the many hours when I had been forgotten and wandered about lost on that first day in my new home. I could blame the sheltie dog, named

Lightning, who ran me up the tree on my first day venturing outside. Or, maybe I had become accustomed to having a litter box again, and found it more accessible than searching for my space outdoors. Whatever the reason, it was an easy and painless transition. The Mistress and Miss Ticiana understood and respected my wish to spend most of my time indoors.

This is not to say that I did not survey my world from my outside balcony, which overlooked the entire estate. From the ledge of the balcony, located adjacent to our kitchen, I could sit and enjoy the vast grounds, the pond, swimming pool and tennis courts. I befriended a blue jay and tried unsuccessfully to discourage a noisy crow from making its nest in the tree on the porch. The tree had been there when the house was built, so they simply built the porch around it. The porch was built on stilts so my vantage point was quite high, and you know that cats love heights. The Mistress once explained this to her daughter within my hearing. She said that thousands of years ago Siamese cats were used as watch cats on the high walls of temples and palaces. Evidently, that is why we cats search for the highest lofts to explore and on which to relax.

So I teased Lightning from my high command post, and he had enough sense to never climb up the steps. Lightning belonged to June, Marke, Shawne and Nicke, and this family soon became very dear friends of our family. Lightning and I, however, only tolerated and teased each other. Whenever I wanted to descend from my balcony, I made sure that all the dogs living in the compound were nowhere to be seen or heard. I also had to avoid the raccoons, a breed of animal native to these parts. We had an entire raccoon family living on our estate and they normally made their appearances at night. Raccoons love to raid garbage cans and can be vicious if confronted. I came in close contact to one and ran up the nearest tree to escape. To my surprise, so did the raccoon! Now that I'm remembering this, perhaps this is my true reason for becoming an indoor cat.

I was now thirteen years old. In human years, perhaps ninety-one! Someone told the Mistress that you must multiply seven human years times each cat's year, so that sounds about right. I felt like a young lady, and my family always complimented me on my youthful appearance. I just realized that I have not even told you what I look like! I am a tabby cat, which is usually a mixture of brown, grey and white. I also have broad black stripes on my back and brown and white fur on my tummy. I truly love having my tummy brushed. All cats have a favorite place to be scratched and brushed, and this is mine.

We had many visitors in our home in Crescent Beach. Miss Ticiana was now attending the University of Oregon, but often returned for vacations and weekends, usually bringing along a friend or two. The Mistress's siblings also came to see us, as well as Cousin Lisa and her daughter Miranda. Miss Cassandra and her husband Dan came over the Christmas holidays. Also Mr. Mike was a constant visitor, which cheered up the household considerably. Other friends came too, and as I overheard conversations about skiing, I realized that this sport drew many people up to the area.

Now that I had become basically an indoor cat, I developed new games where I could engage my psychic skills to the fullest. Whenever a visitor entered our house, I quickly realized that I could figure out several things about him. First, I picked up his aura, or field of energy. From this, I could find his vibrations. I knew whether he was likely to make sudden movements or loud noises. From the smell, I knew what sort of animals he kept in his home. To discover these and other deductions, I simply employed my four avenues of investigation: eyes, ears, nose and whiskers. At this point, I decided whether I would accept him. If I chose not to accept this person, I tried to realize what he expected from me. Then I would do just the opposite! I am the first to admit that the feline can be quite unpredictable!

I would also let guests know my place in the household. When they were all settled in the living room and warming themselves by the fire, I would quietly arrive and survey the situation. Then I tiptoed haughtily across the carpet with my welcoming "mrrrrrow," making a routine inspection of the sofa, the visitor's shoes, the table, and the remains of cheese and crackers. Once I was satisfied with everything I selected my place close to the fire and stretched out in my tigress pose. I then might extend my front paws in front of me, push out my neck and yawn. At this point, I would probably accept any guest that I felt drawn to, and allow him to adore me with stroking and praises until I fell asleep.

Various indoor and outdoor dinner parties were held in this house and I would time my appearances cleverly. After I was satisfied with observing, I would move on to my "obtaining information" routine. My eavesdropping was accomplished while pretending to be asleep. This is how I learned at the Thanksgiving dinner that the Mistress and Mr. Mike were planning to buy a house in this area! At the Christmas dinner, I discovered that they were getting married! That bit of news jarred me right out of my listening position (sitting tall on the top step, tail curled around my front paws and eyes sparkling in the firelight). I jumped right into the Mistress's lap to show my approval! Finally, one warm summer afternoon at an outdoor pig roast, I discovered that Mr. Mike had finally received his transfer to the Washington border! It appeared that everything was fitting into place after all!

In a cat's eyes, all things belong to cats.

English proverb

The Good Life

We lived in and enjoyed our wonderful expansive rental home in Crescent Beach for ten months. I know this time line because I heard ten months mentioned during one of my eavesdropping moments with the family. A cat has no idea of time, but humans love to measure things in days, weeks and months, so we go along with their habits. Apparently the house in which we lived was a "summer home" for the owner family, and the Mistress was well aware of the situation when we moved in. So after ten months she knew she had to leave. She was prepared to do so.

The Mistress and Mr. Mike became engaged to be married shortly after our arrival to Canada. I noticed a beautiful diamond ring on her hand, which I sniffed and licked, causing her to laugh and tell me about the proposal. He was still trying to get his transfer through U.S. Customs to the northern border so they could live together after their marriage. After learning of this, I again placed a white light around their persons, their marriage, and their wishes. I was not a bit surprised when she excitedly proclaimed that his transfer had come through!

Although I was not consulted on the selection of the new house, I know that my welfare was considered. They chose a lovely home with a fenced-in back yard, a deck, and a hot tub, which provides me with many moments of warmth sitting atop and sleeping. There is a pear tree next to the hot tub, which is the best place I have ever found to sharpen my claws. The only drawback is the dog next door, called Kebo. She basically leaves me alone, but she loves to stake claim to her territory. I find that I can get along well with her because I stay in my area and she usually stays in hers.

The Mistress and Mr. Mike married that summer in Washington state, with all the family and friends in attendance. Miss Cassandra, Miss Ticiana and I were very happy for them, because we knew that they would be wonderful partners. I, of course, could not attend the wedding, but graciously received all the relatives who visited us after the event. The summer passed by quickly. We all enjoyed our new home and the space it allowed for relaxation and peace.

Even more friends and family have paraded through this house since that summer! The attraction must be the beach. We live just two blocks from the beach, and I've discovered that I can sit and watch the ocean from the master bathtub. What a delight to focus in on the Mistress and Mr. Mike as they jog along the beach or walk together down the Promenade to have dinner. It makes my heart smile to see that they are fulfilling their dreams.

Miss Ticiana spends the summers here, working as a service rep for a local cruise line. She often invites her young friends to the house for a barbecue, which is always fun because they cook up tender pieces of chicken or beef. My mouth waters when I inhale the aromas, and Miss Ticiana always makes sure I get my proper share.

Miss Cassandra and Dan also visit us, so there are times when the entire family is under one roof! Those are very happy times for me! Just the three of us live a very peaceful life. I am now an "only child" and have become even more spoiled. My food selection has become more varied, and the brushing sessions have increased. I also have a novel form of entertainment: the Mistress recently read a book about cats that paint. She bought me paint and set up a room for me to express myself through the art of painting. I did attempt it once, but found the paint to be too sticky and messy for my taste. So they shifted their interest and began to talk about future trips. I heard that a new cat carrier would be purchased to include me in these activities. I hope that someday I will learn to enjoy car trips.

In the meantime, I'm very content with our family of three. Each night after they fall asleep, I arise from my "assigned" place at the foot of the bed, stretch and yawn and journey to the front end, nosing my way under the covers. Working to the foot of the bed I snuggle close to two bodies, and there I sleep peacefully. By morning I am usually found with my head on one of the pillows, covered by blankets and nestled against a warm body. Some days I awake sprawled crossways on the bed, only to discover that both of the masters seem to be clinging to the edges of the mattress, searching for space. It is, indeed, a cat's world!

He lives in the half-lights in secret places, free and alone—this mysterious little-great being whom his mistress calls "My Cat."

Margaret Benson, English writer

Earthquake

As I have told you, cats can return to their friends and adventures through dreams of past times. Sometimes we do this when we are not fully sleeping, but want to revisit our memories. That is what a "cat nap" can do for us. If I'm stretched out, warm and lazy but not really sleepy, I will evoke a special thought and relive it for my pleasure. I often do this with my youthful days in Mexico, bringing the young ladies back as children and romping through carefree adventures with Canica. Once in a while these remembrances are not pleasurable, yet come unbidden to disturb me during one of these quiet moments.

Canica and I were almost two years old, still adolescents and very mischievous young cats. We were enjoying ourselves early one school morning while Miss Cassandra and Miss Ticiana were upstairs getting dressed. They had misplaced their backpacks and were laughing together searching for them. The Mistress was downstairs preparing breakfast, and we could hear her quietly discussing the day's activities with Señorita Teresa, our live in housekeeper. Both Canica and I were biting and swatting at the girls' shoelaces in an effort to get their attention. Suddenly, without any warning, we felt a movement and heard a far away rumbling beneath the earth! Because cats sit so close to the ground we notice things before humans. We knew then that the first rolling of the earth had begun! Canica stopped in his tracks, reached out to me and instinctively lowered his head. I also sank to the floor and peeked up at Miss Ticiana, who was closest to me, to see what she would do. For those first few seconds, neither child appeared to notice.

In one horrifying instant we all heard the crash of dishes below. I looked up to see the ceiling lamp swaying while the bedroom shelves slowly began to slant toward the floor. Canica crawled between Miss Cassandra's legs before she bent her knees to keep her balance. She remarked to Miss Ticiana that she felt very dizzy. What was happening?

We heard the sound of the Mistress's footsteps rushing up the stairs. She grasped their hands and gently but firmly guided them down the stairs, just as the second jolt forced them backwards onto their buttocks! Miss Ticiana began to whimper while Miss Cassandra nervously queried her mother about the situation. Canica and I scampered under the bed. We watched from under the dust ruffle as the Mistress calmly took charge, explaining to the girls and to Señorita Teresa that they must go quickly under heavy furniture, such as their dining room table, or stand beneath the doorway. Moments later we heard loud sounds of cracking and the popping of the electrical lines.

Slowly and deliberately, hand in hand, they proceeded down the remaining stairs until the three of them and Señorita Teresa stood under the massive front doorway. From there they listened to the car radio announcing an earthquake and advising people to stay in their homes. Absorbed by the news, they

were suddenly jolted out of their concentration by the shrill ringing of the telephone. The Mistress went back inside to answer and spoke quietly with the Master, who was already at work. She assured him that we were fine and that she would keep the girls home and ensure our safety. The phone line went dead as she was speaking to him, and all power ceased. Now our only news would come through the car radio.

Canica and I remained huddled together under the bed where we experienced the after-shocks, or tremors. They were very frightening because we could do nothing but roll with the movements. I was proud to observe that the Mistress kept all of them calm by explaining what was happening and how we would all be fine as long as we stayed in a safe spot. The girls wanted to know that we cats were also safe, so the Mistress returned to the bedroom to pull us out from under the bed.

We all sat quietly together for a long time, listening to the news and becoming more saddened and surprised as we heard the many repercussions from this terrible incident. At some point we discovered that it measured 8.1 on the Richter scale, making it one of the largest earthquakes ever to be recorded!

Days later we heard that more than 8,000 people were killed and thousands of homes were destroyed. Five hundred hotels and high rise buildings crumbled and fell, while other parts of the ground simply opened up, sinking everything around them! The Mistress told us that the amount of damage to Mexico City was estimated to be around four billion dollars! This was a shocking tragedy. We were among the fortunate. This helpless feeling of living through an earthquake sometimes returns to haunt each one of us.

Warmth

I awake with a jolt from the earthquake dream. Looking around me, I find I'm outside on the deck next to the hot tub, and it's very warm. My fur feels baked, and my mouth is dry. I stretch lazily and walk slowly to the back door, where I sit patiently, looking wistful. The Mistress notices me after a few moments and rushes to let me into the house.

Cats love warmth. We will go to great lengths to find warm places. Even though we have fur coats, our ventilation system is such that we feel the cold when we're outdoors on a cold or windy day. My heart goes out to my homeless cat brothers and sisters who live in frigid areas. Imagine trying to wash off icicles from soggy fur!

Until we moved to Vancouver, British Columbia I had only experienced temperate climates. Mexico City was almost always warm, with an occasional cold night during the winters. San Diego, while being a coastal area, did not have cool moisture clinging to the air. Once in a while we had a cold day or night, but I was always safely tucked away indoors sunning myself on a window ledge. But Vancouver's air is moist and often cool, due to the inordinate amount of rain that falls from November to April. It was in Vancouver where I chose to become an indoor cat.

But I digress again. I was speaking to you of warmth. This is a topic of great interest to cats when we socialize. During those many hours a day when we sleep, we often dream up novel ways of maintaining that heated state of perfect bliss. I will share with you my favorite methods of staying warm, perhaps providing new ideas to any of you cats who may be listening while my story is read aloud.

Naturally the sun provides our greatest source of heat, and we will find the only strip of sunshine available if necessary. Fortunately, the sun has been there for me throughout my life (except some days during the wintertime in Vancouver) so I just stretch out and slumber, following the sun as it passes overhead and alights in different rooms of the house. Heaters and furnaces and fireplaces also provide warmth, but the feeling is not quite as fulfilling and as satisfactory as is the sun.

Curling up in bed next to warm bodies is deliciously comforting, as you share the heat right from the source. I particularly like to wiggle under the covers to the foot end of the bed and wrap myself around legs and feet. Sometimes I can sleep for hours before having to come out for fresh air. I also like to sleep between bodies, squeezing myself quietly in between buttocks and tummies. When I get too hot, I move on up to the pillows and nestle in next to warm hair. The Mistress sometimes tells me that I become annoying, especially when I shed my fur on the pillow. But I'm still sleeping in the bed!

Another wonderful source of warmth is a waterbed. I slept on one every night while we lived in San Diego. Both Miss Cassandra and Miss Ticiana had waterbeds, turned up to a blissfully warm temperature. Canica and I took turns moving from one bed to another, or often sharing one bed with each girl.

Those were glorious nights to be sure! Unfortunately the Mistress sold those waterbeds when we moved north.

If the house feels cold and nobody is around, I recommend slipping into the back of a dresser drawer and making a nest among sweaters, socks, underwear, or nightgowns. You can sleep undisturbed for hours and are surrounded by the natural heat that clothing gives off once warmed by your body. You will feel "snug as a bug in a rug," as my Mistress loves to say.

I do not recommend running or any other form of exercise to achieve warmth. This is what humans do,

and having tried it I found it tiring and boring. We cats are more clever and can become warm with far less exertion.

Oh, one last word of caution: don't look or act like you are cold. They will come forth with a sweater of some kind. I was fitted into a sweater once and my dislike was so obvious that it never happened again. If you find the outdoors too cold for comfort, become an indoor cat!

The cat seldom interferes with other people's rights. His intelligence keeps him from doing many of the fool things that complicate life.

Carl Van Vechten, American writer

Please Welcome Jasper!

L iving in Canada has been a real treat for my senses of sound and smell. There are totally different flowers here than I experienced in Mexico or San Diego, and these are sweet and fragrant. The flowers begin to blossom in mid to late March, filling the air with the fresh odors of spring. Because we live close to the bay, the air in our back yard is heavy with the flavor of salty sea breezes. At first, the squawking and shrilling of the seagulls and crows flying overhead awakened my sense of the chase, but now I just enjoy hearing them arguing and making up.

About three years ago, just as spring was bursting into summer, I realized that I was lonely. The Mistress and Mr. Mike worked long hours, and then often traveled on their days off. Of course they made sure I had my food and proper attention while they were gone, but I could not share my days. I did have some friends in the neighborhood who always visited my place. Because I disliked wandering over the fence into other people's yards, my social outings were limited.

What I missed the most was snuggling against Canica. The fur on a cat is so soft, so warm and toasty and so comforting that it cannot be replaced with fireplaces, wool, down comforters or even the human skin. I really never considered the idea of my family adopting another cat, but I longed for a close buddy. Perhaps I missed the girls, who were grown up and far away. Miss Ticiana still visited us frequently but Miss Cassandra and Dan lived in Minnesota where she was attending law school. As much as I wanted to see them, I did not want another airplane ride, and certainly not a car ride from one country to another!

What I wanted was a reliable friend: someone who

lived with me, played with me, and shared our home and lives. Maybe I was yearning for the equivalent of what marriage is to humans. I was fifteen years old, healthy, energetic, and lonely. How could I share this yearning with the Mistress and Mr. Mike? It is possible, and I will show you how this worked for me.

I am very fortunate because my favorite human, the Mistress, has always adored cats. She was raised with cats and learned very early on how to communicate with us. She never spoke down to a cat, but on our level, explaining everything to us so that we could use our intelligence to project a part of ourselves into humans. Because she could imagine a part of herself into a cat, we could communicate without words, but with silent observations. For example, by watching her demeanor I knew when she was sad, joyous, fearful or uncertain. She knew when I was restless, melancholy, or playful. And she also knew when I finally realized that I wanted a companion.

She and Mr. Mike were planning a three-week trip to Europe. I knew this from listening to their conversations and although the time frame of three weeks meant nothing to me, I observed that they were very hesitant to leave me under the care of neighbors for such a long time. They discussed solutions to this problem and began talking about bringing another cat into the household. In the beginning, they realized that I felt uneasy and jealous during those conversations. The Mistress watched me closely and talked to me about this. I slowly began to understand that this would resolve my loneliness and bring me a companion. As I warmed to the idea, they realized that it was my wish to share my home with another cat!

When the time came to select a kitten they contacted the local Humane Society. They were given the name of a woman who takes into her home the older kittens and cats with little chance of adoption. From what I heard, this lady houses over thirty kittens and cats and is successful in finding families for many of them. They agreed to choose an older kitten and went to visit the woman to discuss their plan. The next day, the Mistress, Mr. Mike, Miss Cassandra and Miss Ticiana all went to pick out the new family member, while I nervously awaited his arrival! I had no idea of what to expect, but I guess I was envisioning a small kitten, female, eager to meet me and follow me about. What I got was a long, lean, wide-eyed white male with black patches who bolted at the sight of me! Please welcome Jasper!

Educating Jasper

Jasper was a skittish, suspicious male kitten about three months old when he entered into our lives. It appeared that he and his sister had been mistreated, because both kittens were wary of humans. The lady who was housing him urged the family to take his sister as well, which Miss Cassandra and Miss Ticiana considered a wonderful idea. But the Mistress, knowing me well, wisely decided that two new cats would have been more than I could handle. During those first few days I wondered why she had not chosen the female. But she knew that Jasper would eventually protect and pamper me, and she was right on both counts.

Mr. Mike had built a wire fence upstairs, separating Jasper from the rest of the household. He had the run of two bedrooms, a hall and a bathroom with his private litter box, bed and food dish. It was understood that because each of us needed time to become accustomed to each other, we should be separated in the beginning. That worked for me, but not for Jasper! After our brief introduction, during which he hissed at me and I spat back at him, he was taken to his quarters and I went out onto the deck to enjoy the sun. Jasper lasted about fifty seconds before he scrambled up and sailed over the top of the fence. The Mistress and Mr. Mike looked at each other in amazement, and knew they had lost that battle.

So Jasper moved into the household and I was tasked to teach him manners and house rules. As his self-appointed mentor and elder, I took my responsibilities very seriously. First, he needed to respect my position as the "Matriarch." This meant not eating off my plate, not using the joint litter box until I was finished, and never jumping into anyone's lap if I were occupying it. I showed him where he could sharpen his claws, how to apply the "whisker torture" to wake up the masters, and the methodology of training the humans to let us in/out at our whim. These lessons took some time, but Jasper wanted to please. He later told me that he had never experienced such delicious food before and was eager to play by the rules and earn his keep. His attitude pleased me greatly, and I began to see that this just might work out.

I discovered that Jasper was named after Jasper National Park in the Canadian Rocky Mountains. The Mistress and Mr. Mike had visited the area and fallen in love with it, taken photos and made an album. When it came time to name him one of the Mistress's colleagues at work remembered the beauty of the photos and suggested the name. Jasper also has a black heart-shaped patch of fur on his left back leg, so they gave him a middle name, Sela, which means "heart-shaped" in the Lummi Indian language. As you can see, the Mistress spends a great deal of thought and energy on our names. My name, Kiska, means "cat" in Russian and I have always been quite proud of its uniqueness.

Jasper was a quick study and soon we made a good team. He loved to explore the neighborhood and visit with all the cats. He didn't seem afraid of the

dogs either, and actually struck up a guarded friendship with Kebo, the golden retriever who lives next door. Jasper never ran from Kebo when she bounded over to our yard, but stood his ground and watched as Kebo lay down and waited for orders. They would stare each other down, then Kebo would inch closer and Jasper would rise, arch his neck and walk over to rub noses. At this point, Kebo would saunter back home with a bewildered and slightly embarrassed backward glance at Jasper.

For several weeks Jasper slept anywhere in the house at night. I taught him the "whisker torture" game, after which the Masters decided that one cat in the bed was quite enough! The whisker torture is used in the mornings when the humans sleep too late and the cats need breakfast. We hop weightlessly onto the bed and lightly touch our whiskers to their faces, first to the chin and nose. This is usually met with grumbles and an invitation to go away. Then we approach them and go for the more sensitive areas: cheeks, mouth, and eyelids. The humans now must sit up and wake up, and we quickly hop off the bed and out of the room, mission accomplished. I am sorry that poor Jasper paid for this lesson by being banned to the laundry room each night. He doesn't mind, since he has a huge cushioned bed and the warm tops of the washer and dryer from which to keep watch of the outdoor nightly activities.

Jasper grew quickly, and in no time was bigger than me! He loved to eat, and soon became very friendly with neighbors. Jasper quickly understood that he would be given tidbits here and there by being charming. The Mistress and Mr. Mike noticed that he was becoming hefty but attributed it to his growing spurts. Jasper also has

an unusual voice. He can only squeak, making a high pitched "mew" sound. I have tried helping him do the "meooow" noise when hungry, the "yeowl" noise when annoyed and irritated, and the "meup" noise when contented but the poor guy can only produce his mew. Because of that, he doesn't speak vocally to humans, but he does use his large green eyes to express his feelings.

The Masters were about to leave on their long trip, and Jasper and I were ready. We had plans and were actually looking forward to having the neighbors baby-sit us, because we devised methods to get around the regulations that our family had left them. I will relate these to you, and perhaps you will share this next chapter with your cats, who might get some good ideas!

Who can believe there is no soul behind those luminous eyes?

Theophile Gautier, French writer/critic

Pushing the Envelope

It was a very warm September morning and they were packing and rushing about getting ready for their European vacation. Jasper and I watched them with mixed feelings. I knew I would miss them and their care giving, but at the same time I was excited to join Jasper in his proposed adventures during their absence. Jasper had a twinkle in his eyes and was looking forward to this freedom, much like a teenager when his parents go away. The other neighborhood cats had been advised that our house would soon become the social hub for activities.

Finally the departure day arrived. The Mistress

held us and kissed us and told us to be good cats. Mr. Mike hugged us also, and explained again that the next door neighbors would be feeding us, and letting us in and out, and their children would come around to play with us. All sorts of catnip toys and treats had been purchased for this occasion, so our pampering had already begun. Then they were gone! Neither of us understood the concept of "three weeks," but we knew it was a long time for them to be away. The weather was warm, and our yard was fragrant with hydrangeas bursting forth in pillows of bright colors. Jasper and I sat together in our back yard, inhaling the aroma of the salty ocean mist.

Later that morning Jasper led me over the fence to visit two of his buddies on the next block! I had never left our block during my entire stay in Canada, so it took some persuasion on his part to lead me so far from home. We arrived at a woodsy area next to a ravine, where Zombie and Biscuit lived. Zombie was a longhaired black and white cat, quite similar in coloring to Jasper. He was very large and peaceful by nature. Biscuit was marmalade female, orange and white and kind and sweet to me. I recognized Zombie from back yard visits to our home, but Biscuit was more of a homebody as I am. We spent several hours with them, exploring the riverbed and chasing moles in their large back yard dens. It was fun and I truly enjoyed my outing. We returned home and found the kitchen window open for our convenience. Exhausted, I quickly fell into my favorite sun covered chair for a long sleep.

The neighbors, Bob, Mel, Devin and Ashleigh, came by daily to feed us in the morning and in the evening. During nice weather they left the kitchen window open until late afternoon. They also spent some time playing with us, and would show up unannounced whenever they could. That was how we got busted!

It happened on a peaceful afternoon when all of White Rock seemed to be resting. There was no wind and it was warm, not hot. Because of the balmy weather, Jasper decided to invite all the neighborhood cats over to visit. There were about 10 of us sprawled out in the house, plus a special treat: a large mouse proudly presented by Zombie for our entertainment pleasure. We took turns chasing the creature through the house until finally we became bored and decided to release him. As we lay relaxing in the sun covered family room, some dozing of, others playing with the catnip toys, we felt a new presence alighting on the open windowsill. A large shabby black cat had found his way to our house, probably enticed by the scent of food. As he gingerly entered through the open kitchen window and crept toward the food bowl, several of us sat upright and growled. Some began to edge their way towards him, with ears back and eyes narrowed. I watched as Jasper, in the role of master of the household, approached him with a savage growl. The black cat went up over the table and around the chair with Jasper and several others in pursuit.

At that very moment Ashleigh and Devin opened the back door, just in time to witness the black cat ducking under the kitchen table and Jasper sailing over it. Another cat skidded on spilled water and sent the bowl flying! All of us were now awake and enjoying the spectacle. The startled children had encountered a circus of felines, some in chase, others posing as a captive audience. They stood silent and still as all the neighboring cats flew out the door right past their startled faces. I wonder to this day if they told the Masters!

It is impossible for a lover of cats to banish these alert, gentle, and discriminating little friends, who give us just enough of their regard and complaisance to make us hunger for more.

Agnes Repplier, American essayist

12
Differences

Anyone who has been owned by cats or has loved cats knows that every cat is unique. My personality is very different from Jasper's, and so are my tastes, moods, desires and physique. While he is hefty, big boned and powerful, I am petite, slim, and dainty. This is not because he is male and I am female. Our neighborhood friend, Cally Calico Cat, is female and she is large, strong and imposing but also feminine and sweet.

When the Masters go to work, we cats have totally different programs for the day. I sleep more than Jasper, probably seventy-five percent of my day. If we are left indoors I will find my morning sleeping spot and settle in early. During the day I follow the sun as it moves through the house and I choose my sleeping sites accordingly. When I awaken I eat, play, bathe, and daydream. At this point, one of them usually comes home and lets us outside, where I can entertain myself for a short while until I feel like reentering the warmth of the house. During the summer I spend much more time outdoors, because it pleases me to feel the sun directly on my fur.

Jasper does things very differently. He always looks for food, and because he has found and raided the dry food bag in the pantry, the Masters have to hide food from him. He is also a window cat. He sits at every window in the house and does surveillance. He has his morning windows, from which to enjoy morning activities in the street, and his afternoon spots. Usually the other cats come around in the afternoon, so Jasper holds court from his window throne in the family room and makes plans for later when he is let out. One of his favorite spots around noontime is the computer monitor upstairs, from where he can survey half our block and over to the next street.

Jasper sleeps about half the day. Maybe this is

because he sleeps all night long in the laundry room but I doubt it, because he has a window in there also. Miss Cassandra has complained to the Mistress that it is unfair that Jasper has to sleep behind closed doors, but I know for a fact that when they are gone and he could sleep anywhere, he still goes to his bed in the laundry room. If he's especially tired during the day he will go to his laundry room bed. He has never complained to me that I get the bed with the Masters and he has to sleep in his own room.

Jasper is the leader and I am the follower, when I choose to follow. I was also the follower with my brother Canica. I am rather timid and shy around animals, but not so with people. A few years back I preferred not being held and squeezed by small children, but no longer. In my older years I have learned to enjoy the pampering. Jasper, however, is frightened by children and will try to escape when he hears their footsteps or voices. I think he was teased and taunted by younger people when he was very small, but he doesn't remember much from that time of his life. So when it comes to people skills, Jasper learns from me!

He is also an adventurer and will disappear for hours searching out other cats or taking long walks.

He loves rooftops, and will jump from one to an-other, just for the fun of it! He also sunbathes on rooftops, particularly our own. He scales over fences with the greatest of ease, while I sit below and watch him. Sometimes he is chased by a dog and allows the dog to catch up to him. Just as the dog is about to nip at Jasper's heels, he takes one gigantic leap up and over the fence. The dog screeches to a stop, totally baffled by what he has just seen. Jasper is an athlete and a doer, while I am a thinker and a planner.

The cat, like the genius, draws into itself as into a shell except in the atmosphere of congeniality, and this is the secret of its re-markable and elusive personality.

Ida M. Mellen, American writer

O Canada!

All of us were really enjoying our lives in Canada. Jasper was our true Canadian, but the Mistress and I joked about taking the best of wherever we lived and adapting it to our personalities. For example, she began to pronounce certain words the Canadian way, such as "again, schedule, progress, laboratory:" words written the same but sounding very different. Canadians are very courteous and civilized, and I rather enjoyed observing the custom of the humans' removing their shoes whenever they entered a house. Jasper and I often joined Mr. Mike as he watched hockey games on the television, a sport I had never seen before. Canadians like soccer too, which pleased me greatly. It reminded me of the afternoons I shared with the Master, Miss Cassandra and Miss Ticiana watching the World Cup when it played in Mexico some years ago. All of this was new for Jasper, and he reveled in learning and participating.

Jasper was now fully grown and very handsome. His long white fur glistened, set off by the black patches. He had a very long tail that he could wrap all the way around his paws and over to his other side. His green eyes sparkled and twinkled whenever he thought up a new scheme. One afternoon he wanted to paint on the Canadian Inuit statue that the Masters kept on display in the family room. I had to explain to him that one does not paint over the work of an artist! Fortunately the Mistress had not set up the paints anywhere near the statue.

During the past summer, Miss Ticiana and Ted had married! They visited us often because they lived in Oregon, which is rather close. Also, Miss Ticiana was working for an airline and enjoyed free passes to fly wherever she wanted! Miss Cassandra and Dan and their baby, Marlena Grace, visited us as well so I spent time with all of my loved ones. How charming it was to have a baby in the house! Perhaps I am biased, but she is truly a beautiful baby! The funny thing is that a few years back I would have hidden under the bed if ever I heard a baby cry. Now Jasper has taken on that role. One time the Master came up here from Mexico and spent several days with us! It was wonderful to hear his voice and feel his hands rubbing my tummy and petting my head.

As promised, the Mistress and Mr. Mike took us for short rides in our new car carriers. They wanted to teach Jasper from an early age to enjoy the car. It worked for him. It still bothered me, especially if they forgot to bring my littler box along. But we accompanied them, and actually visited some beautiful places and enjoyed even more of beautiful British Columbia, including Vancouver Island.

One afternoon we were lifted into our soft-sided carriers and placed on the floor of the back seat of the car. Jasper settled right in and I immediately began to protest. Finally I was released and allowed to sit on the Mistress's lap. This is how I was able to see us drive onto a very large floating boat, called a ferry. We parked next to other cars and were carried upstairs to enjoy the boat trip. Naturally we had to stay in our carriers, but we could see the ocean and other

ships passing, which was a first for both of us! We were well behaved during the moments we were allowed to stay on deck, because it was exciting.

The ferry docked and all the cars drove off. It was at this point that I guessed we still had a long ride to go, but again I was allowed to sleep on the Mistress's lap so I did not complain. Jasper lay calmly in his carrier on the back seat. Finally, we arrived at a cabin in the woods in an area that looked remarkably like the forest around my Mexican weekend home in Valle de Bravo. This lovely place is called Tofino, and from what the Mistress told us it is located on the farthest western coast of Vancouver Island. Jasper and I were released inside the cabin and immediately set out to explore. It smelled wonderfully of burnt logs and pine trees. How it reminded me of Valle de Bravo, my brother Canica, and the young girls! Jasper and I loved it, and spent that night snuggled next to our family, listening to the waves breaking against the rocks.

The next day we ventured out onto the deck. It was a sunny day and the air was crisp. From the deck we could see the ocean! As long as the Mistress and Mr. Mike were out there with us, we could walk around the area and smell everything. What a glorious morning it turned out to be! New sounds greeted us: chirping and warbling birds, the pounding of a woodpecker, distant barking dogs, crashing waves. Neither of us was frightened by the new surroundings and enjoyed them all morning long, while the Masters read and sun bathed. When they set off to explore the area, we were taken back into the cabin, where we spent a peaceful afternoon lazing in the sun.

That evening we all shared special moments in front of the fire. We were brushed, read to and adored, which is what we like best. Later that night Jasper captured a mouse and made a great deal of noise playing with it up in the loft. Mr. Mike got out of bed to terminate that nonsense. The next day we again ventured outdoors and later slept on the deck. We were fed the leftover pieces of their delicious meals, in addition to our own food. When we headed back home I silently agreed with the Mistress that it was well worth the inconvenience of the car trip and carrier. When they know we will love the location, they include us in their getaway weekend. Traveling has turned out to be better than I ever imagined!

14

Jasper's Downfall

Spring arrived slowly, following a dreary winter with too much rain. The air was finally warming and we were enjoying more hours of daylight. Jasper and I each did our own things while the Masters were working. But we welcomed them home as a unit. Relying on our sly senses of humor, we devised a plan of action. After only days of practice we polished it to near perfection.

The moment we heard the garage door opening we jumped into action. I would amble into the kitchen and sit perfectly straight by our bowls, tail curled to the right and head held high. With a grunt,

Jasper would then jump down from the window sill and join me. Side by side we would sit in identical positions, waiting for either or both of them to appear. As they greeted us, we would stare into their faces, throwing them patient yet anxious glances. All the time we would look back and forth between them and our empty food dishes. I would offer them my dignified "yeow," and Jasper would then get up and rub between the legs of whoever was getting our food.

He would narrow his eyes, closing them to make "moon eyes" (slits of catly ecstasy) until the aromas of our dinner wafted through the kitchen.

I had noticed that Mr. Mike and Jasper seemed to have a special relationship, just as I have with the Mistress. Jasper followed him around whenever he did outdoor lawn work or made barbecue preparations. Mr. Mike was the one who most often brushed us and clipped our nails, followed by long moments of petting and kitty treats. He bought us a laser pointer and spent many moments urging us to chase it up and down the walls. Mr. Mike is a very calm and gentle man, helpful and caring. He is playful with us and also with the Mistress, and I like to think that Jasper identifies with him.

Because the sound of the garage door opening indicated their arrival, Jasper associated it with food. He would often be playing outside when they arrived and would rush in through the garage ahead of the car. The Mistress worried that they had to be very careful, because Jasper frequently ran ahead in front of the car and then rolled over on the garage floor to show his contentment. They were both careful about driving slowly into the garage, always watchful for Jasper. Sadly, Jasper's endearing manner of greeting turned out to be his downfall.

Mr. Mike had worked many hours and came home tired. As he drove into the garage, he could see Jasper running in front of him so he drove slowly. Somehow, when Jasper rolled over on the garage floor, his long tail stretched out in a direct line with the tire. Mr. Mike felt a sudden thump as he turned off the car. Jasper, totally stunned, bolted out of the garage and into the back yard. He told me later that he felt no pain, only a great deal of pressure on his tail. Mr. Mike searched for him and eventually found him hiding under a bush. He took him into the house and examined him. Jasper's dazed look motivated Mr. Mike to immediately take him to the

vet. Unfortunately it was late now and our vet had gone home. Another vet examined him and told Mr. Mike to take him home and observe him for a day. When he came back to me I tried to comfort him, washing inside his ears with my long pink tongue. But Jasper was in shock, and only wanted to be alone.

That evening, after hearing the story, the Mistress hurried home from work. She and Mr. Mike found Jasper under the bed. She looked into his pain glazed eyes and began to cry. Jasper wanted to console her but could not, and she understood. The next morning Mr. Mike took him back to see our veterinarian. He diagnosed a ruptured spinal tailbone and immediately gave him a time-released medication through a needle in his neck. Within the hour, Jasper no longer felt pain and slowly returned to his sweet self. All of us had suffered terribly during those 24 hours, especially Mr. Mike, who assumed all responsibility and blamed himself.

Within two days Jasper was back to normal, except for his tail. No matter what he tried to do, the thing just hung behind him like a limp rope. He felt as if he were lifting it, but only the portion of the tail closest to his body would move and the rest just dragged. He could still climb fences, leap over objects and shimmy up trees, but the tail would flop limply behind him. The vet had told the Masters to observe Jasper closely to see if his tail impaired his movements. The Mistress reported to him that it did not and we all hoped that the rupture would heal, which was a small possibility. I saw the Mistress's tears and heard her praying aloud with Jasper in her arms. Later that evening I went to Jasper and told him we should pray. He asked me how, and I said:

"You just jump in and do it. Something like this. You can say it with me. Our Father, be with my buddy, Jasper. Help him to get healed, help him to be brave, and to trust You. Amen."

Jasper sat solemnly and looked at me with huge sad eyes. He did not think his tail would heal, but he wanted to accept the lifelessness of it and carry on as best he could. So we prayed again and asked that whatever happened, he would be able to cope.

He was returned to the vet's office and after another examination, the vet suggested that his tail be bobbed. Then he would not have to drag a lifeless appendage any longer. The Mistress was very concerned that he would miss it, or imagine a phantom tail, or be unbalanced without it. The veterinarian assured her and Mr. Mike that he would not remember it after it was gone. He would not miss it, nor would it affect his balance. With very heavy hearts, they hugged Jasper tightly and accepted the verdict of surgery.

Cats know how to obtain food without labor, shelter without confinement, and love without penalties.

W.L. George, American writer

The Elizabethan Cat

Jasper entered the hospital with a long tail and came home with a cone. In the place of a tail he had a bandaged stump. He also wore a plastic cone around his neck, causing him great discomfort and embarrassment. This cone gave him tunnel vision, meaning he could only see directly in front of him, so at first he bumped into everything and constantly startled himself. The poor boy becomes spooked easily anyway, so imagine how confused he became when he banged into walls and furniture. I hurried to his side and guided him around until he got his bearings again.

This large "Elizabethan Era" looking cone was put on him so he would not bite or tear his stitches nor pull off the bandage. He looked really silly in it, with his wide green eyes and bewildered expression, but I did not let him know that. The Masters removed it when he ate and gave him some time with it off so he could bathe himself and they could brush him. They had to watch him closely because just when he thought they weren't paying attention, he went straight for the tail and the bandages. After they were removed, he tried to rip out the stitches and scratch his stump, which itched badly. I wanted to help him, but they watched me closely too. The first few days were hard for all of us, especially for Jasper.

After about a week they let him outside and stayed with him, ever watchful. He still climbed over the fence and into the neighbors' yards so they chased after him and brought him back home. He also climbed up and raced down his favorite trees. All this he did while wearing the cone, so he had obviously become accustomed to it. I washed him a lot and tried to pamper him, but he assured me that he was fine. He had no pain, no phantom tail to haunt him, and still he maintained his balance. If he were humiliated by the loss of his long beautiful tail, he never said so. And I never asked.

One afternoon Mr. Mike took Jasper out on our deck in the back yard. He lay on a lounge chair and began to read while Jasper cooled off in the flowerbeds and I wandered under the deck. Soon I heard the scraping of the cone against the fence, which meant that Jasper had hurdled over it. I emerged from under the deck to find

Mr. Mike fast asleep, and Jasper gone! I jumped up onto Mr. Mike's stomach to awaken him, and watched him as he realized that his charge had disappeared!

With a cry of alarm, he jumped up from the chair and rushed out of the yard. Several minutes later he returned looking very confused. Apparently he had no idea as to where to look for Jasper. Just then the ring of the telephone startled us. As luck would have it, Jasper had wandered into someone's yard on his outing. Because he wore a collar and a nametag, the man was able to notify us. He began the conversation like this:

"Hello. Do you have a large cat that wears a cone? Oh good, because I found him in my back yard. He's fine and seems to be very friendly. What's that? Oh, I live on Phoenix Ave. Oh my gosh! He's traveled about seven blocks with that cone! It's amazing that nothing happened to him, because he can only see straight ahead. Yes, I'll hold him until you arrive."

So Mr. Mike carried Jasper home those seven blocks. Jasper has never told me what was said, but I'm sure they had a very enlightening conversation during that walking episode!

The Cat Council

As I have told you, I decided to become an indoor cat after being left outside all day when we moved into our house in Crescent Beach. Of course I spend time in my own back yard, and I often join Jasper on his outings when he visits the neighborhood cats, but I prefer the peace and quiet of my home. I do like it when other cats come to visit us, especially when the Masters are working or on a trip so we can show them our hospitality. But there is one occasion when I will leave my area and meet with the other cats. This occasion is called a Cat Council.

A Cat Council is conducted under extraordinary circumstances: a crisis, unusual information to impart, or impending danger. I had only attended one Cat Council in three years, and that was during the year of the mole infestation of White Rock. At the Cat Council we came up with a plan to rid our neighborhoods of the pests, much to the delight of our human families. I think I will save that story for another time.

The Chairman of the Cat Council is Bandit, who resembles Jasper in his coloring and personality. They are very good friends and Bandit is a frequent guest at our house. Bandit has his Cat Committee that spreads the word about future meetings. Of course Jasper is one of those communicators, along with Binky, Sammy, Popeye, Scooter and Yoda.

One particular autumn afternoon, Jasper came home in a tizzy, waking me up and urging me to visit several houses nearby because time was running out. The Council was set for 7 p.m., and it was already 5:30 p.m. I stretched gracefully, jumped up on the windowsill and took off. My first stop was Sasha's house at the end of the block. She agreed to accompany me on my rounds. This was cat business, totally serious and involved.

At 7 p.m. we were assembled in the ravine behind

Zombie's house. The two Siamese, each one from a different home, sat side by side, their blue eyes gleaming with excitement. Longhaired elegant Theo belongs to Joy, a very good friend and coworker of the Mistress. Charming cross-eyed Ding-a-ling lives closer to us and comes by to play with me while the male cats are hunting. Allie and Okie were playfully wrestling, with Sasha, Squirt, Richard and Sweetie Pie looking on. Pepper was searching for Trinka, who had not yet arrived. Suddenly we saw her flying over the creek, long white tail stretched behind while all four paws touched down at once on her elegant landing. I went to sit beside Mulder and Oscar while Jasper headed to the front with Colby, who would be the speaker tonight.

Colby cleared his throat and began his tale. He talked about how so many of us play and even sleep on our roofs. We were all unaware of any danger involved with this habit, so this meeting was called to inform us. Our friend Hobie Cat, who lived two houses away from Colby, had been sleeping on his roof the night before. Hobie Cat is a large white Persian whose contrast of fur and the dark roof made him an easy target to be spotted from above. An owl, perhaps looking for diversion, swooped down and lifted the

unaware cat right off the roof! Hobie let out an enormous roar, which was heard by Colby sitting on his fence, and began to defend himself. Because he was strong and heavy he was able to offset the owl's balance and wrestle free from his grip. But he fell about twenty feet and landed with a thump! The worried family overheard the ruckus and rushed outside to carry him into the house. Several minutes later Hobie Cat was taken to the animal hospital. He's back home now, Colby told us, but very sore and bruised.

We listened silently and realized the implications of the story. No more lazy summer nights relaxing on the roof for Jasper. He looked across the clearing at me and I know he was reading my mind. We made our way home solemnly, each cat lost in his own thoughts. As we reached our house, I gratefully climbed over the fence and in through the kitchen window. Jasper lingered a moment searching skyward, perhaps giving thanks for the warning.

Cats are a mysterious kind of folk. There is more passing in their minds than we are aware of.

Sir Walter Scott, English writer

17
Rain City Cats

It was another Vancouver winter: day after day of rain, grey skies and wet streets. Most cats stayed in their homes the majority of the day. It was dreary and even we cats became melancholy. What can we do all day in the house? The Masters did not want to leave us outdoors when they went to work, so we had to endure at least eight hours shut in the house until they returned. We had to work hard to keep from becoming bored.

Jasper sat at his lookout posts throughout the

house and watched the rain fall. I found the warmest corners of the house and daydreamed, often lulled by the howling winds. During one particularly long winter it seemed that one pacific storm followed another. Sometimes the winds were so strong they broke the branches off the trees. The snapping of the splintering wood pierced my dreams, awakening me from a deep sleep and fragmenting my pleasant fantasies.

Jasper would become restless and stage attacks on me. He didn't care that I was daydreaming and revisiting my youth, or talking to Canica in my mind. He would wait until I looked very relaxed, eyes closed and body curled into a ball, and then he would rush at me, landing lightly on my back or tail. My eyes would fly open and I would begin to growl very softly, warning him away. This was an exciting game to Jasper, so he would ignore my advice and the swatting would begin. Because he is twice my size Jasper batted at me gently and playfully. Being so much smaller, I fought seriously to retrieve my peace. Finally, I would run to a hiding spot, small enough for me to crawl under but too small for him to follow.

When I wanted to play chase I would jump on his

sleeping form and begin to run around the downstairs. Jasper would happily follow me and then we would build up speed, sometimes knocking small objects over in the process. We would chase each other upstairs and fly over the beds, competing to see who could leap the highest. Jasper usually won, so I then had to pin him down in a cat stronghold to end the game. When he got too rough, I bit him gently.

One of Jasper's most endearing characteristics was his comical posture, which was often captured in photos. He loved to lay flat on his back, all four feet facing skyward, and look puzzled as to how he arrived in that position. Then he wanted Mr. Mike or the Mistress to rub and scratch his belly and tell him how beautiful he was. It was such an endearing and amusing pose that he could convince anyone that he just happened to land there, circumstantially. I had never found myself contorted in such a manner so I marveled at his ingeniousness. Every human visitor found this to be very lovable, and Jasper certainly cashed in on it!

Occasionally one of us would get outside in the morning and be far away when the Masters called us. We would then have to spend the day outdoors,

searching for shelter and warmth while the other one sat at the window watching with pity. Our kitchen window has a latch so the window will open, allowing us to come and go as we please while open. During the rainy season it is always closed.

One morning I darted out to breathe in the moist aroma of the pine trees and discovered that I had been left outdoors! Then the downpour arrived and I hurried under the hot tub to keep dry. Several hours later I peeked out and saw Jasper sitting on the back of the sofa searching for me. I was cold and hungry and getting very wet out there. Jasper jumped to the windowsill and began batting the lever with his paw. Then he used his head to push down on it, and suddenly the window opened a crack! Jasper was very surprised and pleased with himself. The window still was not open enough for me to get through, so I stood on my hind legs in the pouring rain and nudged it with my head. Success! I pulled myself up onto the ledge and landed waterlogged on the kitchen floor, where Jasper immediately began licking my fur to dry me off. Unfortunately, we could not close the window. By the time they returned the Masters found a wet floor and a cool kitchen. They looked at us with surprise and an expression of bewilderment. I think they believe to this day that they left the window open!

Although all cat games have their rules and rituals, these vary with the individual player. The cat, of course, never breaks a rule. If he does not follow precedent, that simply means he has created a new rule and it is up to you to learn it quickly if you want the game to continue.

Sidney Denham, English writer

Changes in the Air

nother wet season had passed and we had not rusted! People in this part of the world talk about the rain and rusting a lot. They also use a very odd expression: "It's raining cats and dogs." Why they correlate rain with cats and dogs is puzzling to me, since we both try to avoid it. The Mistress once told me an English tale about cats and dogs that lived on the slanted rooftops of the homes. When it rained they slid down the roofs and jumped onto the ground. This may be the history behind that strange phrase.

Jasper and I love the spring in Vancouver, or at

least in our area of White Rock. Our yard comes alive with bugs and worms and we dig for them with great enjoyment. The trees begin to bloom and their sweet fragrance is invigorating. The voices of the birds arriving from down south mingle with our local species. Everyone is in a good mood because the warming sun awakens our spirits. We cats frolic about the neighborhood making social visits and sleeping as little as possible. It is a glorious time of the year!

Some new people moved in next door, bringing two cats and a dog. The cats immediately hopped up on the fence dividing our homes and we engaged in a "stare down." Like dogs, cats are territorial. We want to be sure that other cats understand our domain, and only after they prove themselves worthy will we share it. It took no longer than two days before Dickie and Stormy were invited into our back yard and we into theirs. Their dog Sambo was another matter. He was part cocker and part terrier and made such a ruckus every time he saw us. We finally acknowledged him. Then his owner did the unthinkable. He began to cut down all the wonderful trees in which we had played and hidden! The gaping holes he left were most unattractive to our eyes as well as to the Mistress and Mr. Mike. Their cats recognized our irritation and agreed that their owner had passed beyond the boundary of "good neighbors."

One warm evening Jasper invited Dickie, Stormy and me to walk with him down to the beach. The beach is about a ten-minute walk for cats and I was feeling lazy, but Jasper insisted that we go. We had to keep to the bushes and woodsy areas because there were many people out enjoying the moonlight. While we were walking the beach we encountered a mother raccoon and her little ones. She made quite a

fuss, but we were not interested in disturbing them. Later we heard, but did not see, some distant coyotes. I had seen many coyotes while living in San Diego, but only two during my time in Canada. Both were loping down our front street at about four o'clock in the morning. The Mistress had just left for work, and they were coming around the corner as she pulled the car out of the garage. I witnessed this from a safe distance through the living room window.

Miss Ticiana and Ted came home for several visits during the late spring and early summer. Jasper and I overheard whispered conversations about "another move." Jasper had no idea what a move entailed so I had to explain it to him. I certainly did not want to be uprooted again and go somewhere else. But the Mistress and Mr. Mike seemed comfortable with this conversation, so Jasper and I decided not to trouble ourselves. There was too much beauty outside and excitement in knowing that months of sunshine were here again. We returned to living the moment: our busy daily activities, entertaining our guests, and enjoying the warmth and glory of summer in Vancouver!

No heaven will not ever Heaven be
Unless my cats are there to welcome me.

Epitaph in a pet cemetery

"On the Bumpedy Road Again"

The days stretched on and we reveled in the lazy summer life style. Through half closed eyes we watched as the family prepared for another move. The Mistress boxed up items and they soon disappeared to a storage facility in Blaine, Washington. Then our lovely piano, upon which I had rested and dreamed, was removed from our home! Ted drove it down to Portland to be given to and enjoyed by the Mistress's niece and nephew, Clara and Marshall.

One day a "For Sale" sign went up in the front yard. Then strange people began to walk through our home. Jasper always darted under the bed while I quietly watched from the sidelines. This was a new experience even for me, and I found it quite entertaining. Jasper and I observed these movements with great interest. After the strangers left, Mr. Mike would sit with us on the sofa; Jasper in his favorite position, flat on his back with front paws curled in a boxing pose, back legs facing skyward. He knew little about the essence of picking everything up and traveling to a new area, a new house, and a new life. So I took on the responsibility of instructing Jasper in the "ways and means" of this family's life style. Because I had undergone it several times before, I believed it was my duty to enlighten Jasper and to pave the way. This did not mean that I liked it any better this time than before, but I had a mission to help us all work through this new event.

We made the neighborhood rounds, explaining to all of our friends that we felt another move was approaching. Because we were so sure of ourselves, we called another Cat Council. We urged them all to be on the lookout for change and to help and support us. All of our neighborhood cat buddies rallied to our request. They promised us that they would do whatever we needed so that this transition could be

accomplished as smoothly as possible. I will forever have great respect and gratitude to our White Rock feline friends for standing by us.

After several months of invasion of our privacy, the Mistress and Mr. Mike seemed to breathe a sigh of relief. Evidently the "right folks" had discovered our home, were very happy with it and were ready to buy. Jasper and I did not fully understand the significance of this transaction, but we decided that it meant that we would have to leave this idyllic lifestyle to which we had become accustomed. Again, I explained to him that it would be fine; the Masters would take excellent care of us and we would end up with something even BETTER than we had now! I relived the moves in my life for Jasper, who listened with ears and soul open to what I had to say. Jasper trusted me and knew I would not mislead him.

The next day we noticed that the large "For Sale" sign had been removed from our front yard. We both guessed that this meant that we had a very limited time to make our rounds and say good-bye to our friends. Again, we had an enormous loyalty to our beloved Masters, and were beholden to them in every way. So off we went: I was the leader this time and Jasper followed me. We visited every cat in our area, and explained to each one that we were on our way to a new life. We did not understand where and we did not care. Wherever the Masters wanted to take us is where we would go. Our complete loyalty and dedication was to them, and we knew they were worthy of our trust.

Cats love one so much—more than they will allow. But they have so much wisdom they keep it to themselves.

Mary E. Wilkins Freeman, American writer

Epilogue

We were off again and this time we did not know where we were going! I think the Masters were keeping the destination from us in order to provide an amusing game. The household goods had left several days earlier in huge moving trailers. We had been living in a hotel for about ten days, which brought back to mind my beginnings in Canada. All of this was familiar to me but totally foreign to Jasper.

So we set off with our family on another car trip to the unknown. We crossed the Washington border into the United States and kept driving. Neither Jasper nor

I knew which direction we were traveling, but after several long boring hours we stopped for the night. It was strange: I no longer protested like I used to about car trips. Maybe it was Jasper's company?

Once I heard the Mistress talking about moving to Georgia, which she said is a long way away. We also overheard Mr. Mike discussing a possible job in the state of Washington, and another in a faraway place called Washington D.C., the capital of the United States. So Jasper and I were clueless, and it was a good and comfortable "space" to be in. We were with our loved ones and we were together. Most importantly, we knew we were about to embark on another totally awesome life adventure!

About the Author

Pamela Bauer Mueller was raised in Oregon and graduated from Lewis and Clark College in Portland, Oregon. She worked as a flight attendant for Pan American Airlines before moving to Mexico City, where she lived for eighteen years. Pamela is bicultural as well as bilingual. She has worked as a commercial model, actress, and an English and Spanish language instructor during her years in Mexico. After returning to the United States, Pamela became employed by the U.S. Customs Service. Presently, she is on foreign assignment with the U.S. government, stationed in Vancouver, British Columbia, Canada. Pamela resides in White Rock, B.C. with her husband, Michael, and their cats, Kiska and Jasper. In the very near future they will return to the United States, where Michael will continue working with U.S. Customs and Pamela will leave the U.S. government service to pursue her writing career.

About the Illustrator

Naomi Marie Weiler was born and raised in the beautiful city of Victoria, British Columbia. This is her second collaboration with Pam and Kiska about the adventures of Kiska, Jasper, Canica and the whole family. She will soon be entering school to pursue a career in set and costume design in theatre. After spending her last summer in Montreal, Naomi has decided to continue her travels and will spend the next summer in Ireland. She dedicates the pictures to Bandit the Terrier, Richard the Clumsy King and to the fond memory of Bobby the Bunny.